Moreno Valley
Public Library
25480 Alessandro Blvd.
Moreno Valley, CA 92553

April 22, 2013

Old MacDonald Had Her Farm

Old MacDonald
Had Her Farm

JonArno Lawson
Art by Tina Holdcroft

annick press
toronto + new york + vancouver

For Sophie, Ashey, and Joseph
—J.A.B.L.

For Nolan and Calum Kraemer and
for William and Bree Holdcroft
—T.H.

Old MacDonald had her farm,
a e i o u.

And when she came across an a,
this is what she'd do:

Saw barn planks, stack sacks.
Sacks fall, stand back
crank cranks, slap backs.

Watch black cats attack fat rats.
Bang at backward taps
grab rags
whack gnats.

Old MacDonald had her farm,

a e i o u.

And when she came across an e,
this is what she'd do:

Get helpers, mend fences.
Bend her knees, feed geese.
Between hen legs—perfect eggs!

Sneeze deep helpless sneezes
then fetch fresh cheeses
where dew-wet trees
meet the sweet bee breezes.

Old MacDonald had her farm,
a e i o u.
And when she came across an i,
this is what she'd do:

Lift pigs
swing picks.
Rip, mix
fix bricks.

Climb, pick, slip!
Lick thick drips
spit big pits!
Trim twigs, snip-snip.

Old MacDonald had her farm,
a e i o u.
And when she came across an O,
this is what she'd do:

Bolt doors, stop hogs.
Toss food to dogs.
Porch lock stops flocks!
Cows chomp on socks.

Mow crops nonstop
from top to bottom or bottom to top.
Look now, too, how bold frog hops—
how crows swoop down off old rooftops!

Old MacDonald had her farm,
a e i o u.
And when she came across a u,
this is what she'd do:

Tug mud-stuck trucks.
Trucks lurch, bulls buck.
Bump-thump rumpus. Ugh! Crunch ...

Munch bunch cut plums.
Clutch hurt thumbs.
Crush spuds, gulp nuts
slurp up lunch.

Old MacDonald had her farm,
a e i o u.
Sometimes she came across a y,
and this is what she'd do:

Spy fly fly slyly by.
Fry, fry. "Fly, fly!"
Pry, dry.
Cry, "My, my!"

Old MacDonald had her farm,
a e i o u.

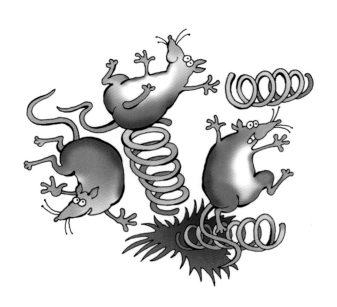

We acknowledge the support of the Canada Council for the Arts, the Ontario Arts Council, and the Government
of Canada through the Canada Book Fund (CBF) for our publishing activities.

ONTARIO ARTS COUNCIL
CONSEIL DES ARTS DE L'ONTARIO

Cataloging in Publication

Lawson, JonArno
    Old MacDonald had her farm / JonArno Lawson ; art by Tina Holdcroft.

ISBN 978-1-55451-457-1 (bound).—ISBN 978-1-55451-456-4 (pbk.)

    I. Holdcroft, Tina   II. Title.

PS8573.A93O54 2012   jC813'.54   C2012-900581-9

Distributed in Canada by:
Firefly Books Ltd.
66 Leek Crescent
Richmond Hill, ON
L4B 1H1

Published in the U.S.A. by Annick Press (U.S.) Ltd.
Distributed in the U.S.A. by:
Firefly Books (U.S.) Inc.
P.O. Box 1338
Ellicott Station
Buffalo, NY 14205

Printed in China

Visit us at: www.annickpress.com
Visit Tina Holdcroft at: www.tinaholdcroft.com